NYLA AND THE DAIRY FREE DISCO

Written by Dominique Thompson
Illustrated by Biva Nguyen

ISBN: 978-1-9196339-0-9

To Nyla, my beautiful daughter, this book is for you.

We have been on a real journey since we discovered that
you have allergies. You have not been
alone on this journey and so this book is dedicated to both
you and your friend, Nyla and Cleo.

To all children and parents on a journey learning to
navigate allergies, you are not alone, it will get easier.

'Mummy, how many days until my birthday?' Nyla asked when they arrived home from nursery.

Mummy held her hand up 'In 5 sleeps!' she replied.

'Yay' Nyla cheered!

'And what's for dinner?'

'Macaroni cheese.'

Nyla rubbed her tummy and licked her lips
'Mmmm' she hummed.

The macaroni cheese was hot, creamy and sticky, just the way
Nyla liked it. She ate it all up.

Soon after, Nyla began to feel all wriggly and just couldn't stop itching. 'What's wrong?' her mummy asked.

Nyla pulled up one sleeve, then the other.

'Look at my arms!' Nyla cried, looking at the skin on her arms.

It had gone all bumpy and was very hot and itchy.

'Oh dear,' Mummy said 'Why don't we try some cream to soothe the itching?'

After a bath, Mummy gently rubbed the cream on Nyla's arms.

'Will it still be my party on Saturday?' Nyla asked as her Mummy tucked her into bed.

'Of course my dear, don't you worry,' Mummy replied.

On Tuesday morning, Nyla was excited to go to nursery.

'How many days until my birthday now Mummy?' she asked.

Mummy held up four fingers 'It's four sleeps now!' she replied.

'Eat your breakfast my love, it's time to leave soon.'

Nyla poured the milk on her cereal and ate it all up.

Soon after, Nyla began to feel wriggly all over again.

'Are you ok Nyla?' Her Mummy asked.

Nyla lifted her t-shirt and looked at her tummy 'I'm all bumpy again!' she cried.

Mummy looked at Nyla's tummy, arms and neck, which had all turned red and were covered in bumps.

'Dear oh dear!' Mummy said.

She found the bottle of cream to soothe the itching and rubbed it all over Nyla again.

'Will it still be my party on Saturday?' Nyla asked as they walked to nursery.

'Of course my dear, don't you worry,' Mummy replied.

On Wednesday after nursery, Nyla and her mummy made their very own pizzas for dinner.

Mummy rolled out the dough and grated the cheese.
'Nyla, you can put the toppings onto the dough.'
'I'm going to make a face!' Nyla shouted excitedly.

She carefully arranged the mushrooms, peppers and olives to make a smiley face.

Nyla was very proud of her smiley pizza and ate it all up.

It wasn't long before Nyla began to feel all wriggly again.
She itched, and she scratched, and she itched some more.
Mummy gasped when she saw Nyla. Her poor skin was bumpier and redder
than ever.

'You poor thing!' she said, giving Nyla a very gentle cuddle. 'I think we need
to take a trip to the doctor in the morning.'

'Will it still be my party on Saturday?' she asked, 'Of course my dear, don't
you worry,' Mummy replied.

On Thursday, Nyla and her Mummy saw Dr Brodie, and she did some tests.

'It appears that Nyla has an allergy to milk.' She explained, 'This is why when you ate macaroni cheese, had milk in your cereal and pizza you got this rash, it's called hives.'

Dr Brodie gave her Mummy a piece of paper from the printer.

'You will need to get a bottle of medicine called antihistamine from the chemist.

If ever you get hot and itchy again after eating something, take some straight away and it will calm the reaction down.'

Nyla looked very worried 'But what about my party on Saturday?' she asked.

Dr Brodie smiled 'You can still have a party Nyla, you will just have to make sure you don't eat any foods you are allergic to, so no milkshakes, no dairy ice cream and no milk chocolate.'

'No chocolate cake!' Nyla wailed. She immediately began to cry.

Mummy gave her a big cuddle.

'Don't you worry, we will just have to find lots of new yummy things to eat for your birthday party,' she said, stroking Nyla's hair.

Yes, you will have to have a dairy free disco!' Dr Brodie clapped her hands in excitement.

Nyla wiped her eyes 'What's a dairy free disco?' She sniffed.

Dr Brodie got a tissue for Nyla and then a leaflet from a rack on the wall.

'There are a few things on this leaflet that look very yummy and they are all free from dairy, so they would be great for a dairy free disco,' Dr Brodie replied.

Nyla looked at the leaflet.

There were pictures of different types of nuts and beans.

'What are these?' she asked pointing.

ALMONDS

OATS

SOY

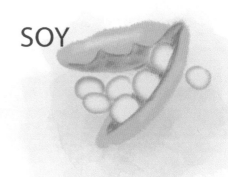

COMMON DAIRY FREE ALTERNATIVES

"Did you know? the most common allergy in children is peanuts and the next most common allergy is to cow's milk."

RICE MILK

COCONUT

'They are almonds, soya beans and coconuts – these are some of the different milks that you can try.'

'This one here is oat milk' Dr Brodie said pointing to a carton on the leaflet.

'I look forward to hearing about your dairy free disco Nyla, please come and tell me all about it!' Dr Brodie said as Nyla and her mummy left her office.

That evening, Mummy tucked her up in bed
and they read a story.

'What if I don't like my dairy free disco?'
She whispered.

Mummy kissed her forehead 'I think you're
going to love your dairy free disco Nyla, just
you wait and see.'

On Friday, Mummy took Nyla to the supermarket.

They went down an aisle that Nyla had not seen before, it was called 'dairy free'.

'We can choose things for your party,' Mummy said.

'I bet there won't be any chocolate cake.' Nyla said sadly

'Don't you worry my love,' her Mummy replied with a smile.

Would you like these cookies Nyla?' Mummy asked.

Nyla thought for a moment. 'Yes please, but they're not chocolate cake.' she said with a sigh.

Mummy put them in the trolley.

'Would you like to get some of these milks? We can use them to make our own special milkshake,' Mummy said.

'Yes please,' Nyla replied with a little smile 'But it's still not chocolate cake' she said and sighed again.

They had almost reached the end of the aisle and Nyla had given up hope of ever having chocolate cake again.
She sat in the trolley and looking down at her shoes.

Just then Mummy asked 'Nyla would you like one of these for your dairy free disco?'

Nyla looked up.

Mummy was holding a big, round, dairy free chocolate cake.

'CAAAAKKKKEE!' Nyla squealed with excitement.

'Is it dairy free?' She asked.

'Yes, it is my love and from now on that's going to be an important question that you will have to ask before you eat something new. Can you remember that?'

'Yes Mummy!' Nyla said dancing in the trolley.

From then on, Nyla asked her Mummy if everything else that went into the trolley was dairy free.

Sometimes Mummy answered and sometimes she asked Nyla to guess.

On Saturday, Nyla sang to herself while pouring her new oat milk on to her cereal.

'Happy birthday to me, Happy birthday to me, Happy birthday dear Nyla, Happy birthday to me!'

Nyla played with her brand-new doll's house while Mummy decorated the living room.

'Nyla, would you like to come and see your disco?' Mummy asked.

'Yes, yes, yes!' Nyla said jumping up and down with excitement.

There were disco lights, glow sticks and lots of balloons decorating the room.

'WOW!' Nyla shouted.

Mummy had made dairy free milkshakes, popcorn, fruit kebabs and in the middle of the table was Nyla's special dairy free chocolate cake.

Nyla hugged her Mummy tightly.

'Thank you, thank you. I love my dairy free disco!' She squealed.

At 2 o'clock the doorbell rang.

It was Nyla's friends Cleo, Albie and Paige from Nursery.

'Welcome to my dairy free disco!' Sang Nyla with excitement.

Mummy put some music on and the children played musical statues.

The doorbell rang again, it was Nyla's Grandma.

She gave her a big hug and kiss.

'Happy birthday Nyla,' she said, 'I bought you some chocolate buttons for you and your friends.'

Nyla thought for a moment and then said, 'Thank you Grandma, are they dairy free?'

Grandma smiled, 'Yes they are sweetheart, Mummy told me all about your allergy well done for checking!'

Nyla kissed her Grandma on the cheek.

'Wow,' she said looking at the shiny packet 'I can even have dairy free chocolate buttons too!'.

THE END.

Printed in Great Britain
by Amazon